U.S. Marines

BY LINDA BOZZO

amicus
high interest

Amicus High Interest is an imprint of Amicus
P.O. Box 1329, Mankato, MN 56002
www.amicuspublishing.us

Library of Congress Cataloging-in-Publication Data
Bozzo, Linda.
 U.S. Marines / by Linda Bozzo.
    pages cm. -- (Serving in the military)
 Includes index.
 Summary: "An introduction to what the US Marine Corps
is, what recruits do, and jobs soldiers could learn. Includes
descriptions of missions to do recon in Afghanistan and
to save Americans trapped in unrest in the Middle East"--
Provided by publisher.
 Audience: Grades K-3.
 ISBN 978-1-60753-392-4 (library binding) -- ISBN 978-1-
60753-440-2 (ebook)
1. United States. Marine Corps--Juvenile literature. 2.
Marines--United States--Juvenile literature. I. Title.
 VE23.B619 2014
 359.9'60973--dc23
                                    2013001414

Editor   Wendy Dieker
Series Designer   Kathleen Petelinsek
Page production   Red Line Editorial, Inc.

Photo Credits
Marine Corps Recruiting Command, cover; Sgt. Christopher R.
Rye/U.S. Marine Corps, 5, 9; Cpl. Courtney G. White/U.S.
Marine Corps, 6; Cpl. Bobby J. Gonzalez/U.S. Marine
Corps, 10; Cpl. Walter D. Marino/U.S. Marine Corps,
13; U.S. Marine Corps, 14, 23; Sgt. Anthony L. Ortiz/U.S.
Marine Corps, 17; Lance Cpl. Heather N. Choate/U.S.
Marine Corps, 18; Cpl. Jonathan Wright/U.S. Marine Corps,
21; Staff Sgt. Ezekiel R. Kitandwe/U.S. Marine Corps, 24;
Staff Sgt. Wayne Campbell/U.S. Marine Corps, 27; Cpl.
Bryan Nygaard/U.S. Marine Corps, 28

Printed in the United States at Corporate Graphics in North
Mankato, Minnesota
5-2013 / 1150
10 9 8 7 6 5 4 3 2 1

Table of Contents

Marine Spy Mission

It is August 2010. The United States has been at war in Afghanistan. A team of U.S. Marines has a mission there. They need to take pictures of the land. They take pictures of people too. Their job is to learn as much as they can. They talk to the people. They look in homes.

 Why were the marines taking pictures?

Marines learn how to use binoculars and scopes.

 They were spying on the enemy. The pictures helped them make maps. Then they learned where the enemy was.

Suddenly, shots fill the air. The enemy is shooting at them! Five marines are hurt. They call for help on the radio. No one answers. The enemy is getting closer. The marines fight to save their lives. They fire back. They use **rifles** and **machine guns**.

Marines know how to use guns to fight against enemies.

Over the shots, they hear helicopters! The marines are running out of bullets. They are hurt. The marines help each other to the chopper. Bullets ring out around them. They climb onto the helicopter. They are safe! They fly back to the base. Doctors can help them now.

A helicopter is ready to
pick up marines.

Helicopters help marines
get to trouble fast.

 Q Does a marine train longer
than other **recruits**?

Learning the Ropes

The U.S. Marine Corps is always ready. They can send out soldiers any time. They are often the first to arrive when help is needed. Marines go all over the world. They know their jobs well. But first they must train hard for 13 weeks.

 Yes! The marines train the longest of all the armed forces. Being ready for action takes lots of training.

Every marine recruit learns to use a rifle. Recruits learn to shoot while standing, sitting, or kneeling. They learn to put **bayonets** on their guns. They do it quickly.

Recruits train hard to be fit. They run. They slide down ropes. They climb over obstacles. Marines are ready for action!

The rope climb is only one part of a marine's difficult training.

Recruits use padded sticks to practice using their bayonets.

What color belt do recruits get?

The U.S. Marine Corps has a Martial Arts Program. It teaches recruits how to fight. They learn how to punch and kick. They practice using bayonets with padded poles. They learn how to use any object as a **weapon**. When they pass, they get a colored belt.

After weeks of training, they graduate. They are called marines for the first time.

 Recruits earn one of five different colored belts to match their skill level. In order, they are tan, gray, green, brown, and black.

Would you like to fly a plane? You could search for the bad guys! On the ground you might drive a Humvee or fire at enemies. You could work on a U.S. Navy ship. You could be on the ground, in the air, or on the sea. But you will be the first to fight. A marine is always ready.

 Why do marines use the navy's ships?

Marines run drills so they can be ready for missions.

 The U.S. Marine Corps is actually part of the U.S. Navy.

These supplies will be taken overseas for a mission.

 Q What gear do marines need?

The Home Front

On the home front, marines train to fight. They also learn to stay safe together. They work as a team to load gear. They must be able to move out quickly. Marines may be called to go overseas at any time. They work to be ready to go.

 They need food and first aid kits. They also need radios, body armor, and weapons.

Marines stay ready for more than just fighting. They help when disaster strikes. After a **hurricane**, marines are there. They drive trucks with tracks that can float. They patrol flooded streets. They search for people who are trapped by the storm. The marines also help clean up and rebuild.

This truck can float on water and drive on land.

Stationed Overseas

In the U.S. Marine Corps, you could work all over the world. Marines fight mostly on land or in the air. They use the navy's ships as bases. This helps them get to trouble quickly. Marines swoop in to rescue soldiers. Marines are never far from the fight.

This marine F-35B jet lands on
a navy assault ship at sea.

A marine uses a metal detector
to sweep for mines.

 How do marines sweep for **mines**?

Marines are usually the first to go into enemy land. They check it out and make sure it is safe. They sweep for mines. These are bombs hidden in the ground by the enemy. If a soldier steps on a mine, it could explode. Marines find the mines before they go off.

They use a metal detector. It shows where metal is buried. They also use a machine called a mine roller. It tests the ground for mines.

The U.S. Marine Corps even help people in other countries. They help after an **earthquake**. They fix buildings. They build hospitals. Marines even help fix roads. They treat people who are hurt or sick. They fly in food, water, and clothes to people. Marines work hard to help and save people around the world.

Marines bring food and water to children in Haiti.

Marines land in New York to
help clean up after a hurricane.

Serving Our Country

It was October 2012. A hurricane hit New York. The streets flooded quickly. People were trapped! Then a fire started. Fire trucks couldn't drive through the flooded streets. Marines to the rescue! Their big trucks drove through the water. They took the firefighters to the burning buildings. They drove the people out to safety. The U.S. Marines are always ready to save people.

Glossary

bayonet A fighting knife that is attached to a rifle.

earthquake When a part of the earth shakes, often causing damage.

hurricane A strong storm over water with high winds and lots of rain.

machine gun A gun that can automatically continue to fire.

mine A bomb that is placed in the ground or in water and set to explode if touched.

recruit A person who has just joined the military.

rifle A long gun that is fired from the shoulder.

weapons Something with which one uses to fight, such as a gun. Marines learn to use many different objects as weapons.

Read More

Goldish, Meish. *Marine Corps: Civilian to Marine.* New York, NY. Bearport Publishing, 2011.

Jackson, Kay. *Armored Vehicles in Action.* New York, NY. PowerKids Press, 2009.

Jackson, Kay. *Military Tanks in Action.* New York, NY. PowerKids Press, 2009.

Sandler, Michael. *Today's Marine Heroes.* New York, NY. Bearport Publishing, 2012.

Websites

Facts about the United States Marines
http://www.usmarinesbirthplace.com/United-States-Marines-facts.html

United States Dept of Veteran Affairs
http://www.va.gov/kids/

US Marine Corps: Marine Recruiting
http://www.marines.com/home

Index

About the Author

Linda Bozzo is the author of more than 30 books for the school and library market. Visit her website at www.lindabozzo.com. She would like to thank all of the men and women in the military for their outstanding service to our country.